To Seth & Dru

♡ Renae
Johnson

The Farmer's Daughter

Renae Johnson

For my husband and daughter. And my wonderfully supportive family and friends. This wouldn't be worth it without you.

Prologue

Jimmy Miller's best friend, Robbie Higgins, turned 17 at 10:47am, June 8th, 1953. Robbie died just before midnight that same day. It was hot, so the pair had spent most of the day by the lake gawking at the local girls. The early evening was reserved for cake and gifts, but the night was for sneaking out.

The light of the harvest moon shone down on a large, old farmhouse and its modest ten acres in the middle of nowhere in Indiana. Jimmy knew the farmhouse belonged to old man Dale Jensen, a hardworking farmer. From one look anyone could see that the farmer's crops were failing, as was his health. His help was gone, as was his wife, Mrs. Jensen. Jimmy remembered his mother making a pie for the farmer when his wife died more than five years ago.

Since then, it was just the old man and his only child, a daughter, Lily. Jimmy wondered how Mr. Jensen could have such a young daughter, she was only 16; he had to be in his seventies.

Jimmy had very little to do with Lily when they'd gone to school together. After her mother's death, Lily had changed. She kept to herself mostly. Her teachers let her shrink into a shell, nearly disappearing altogether.

It wasn't long before her changes were physical. She grew out her dark hair, rarely washed it, and refused to go to school. When she *was* made to go to school, she was thrown out of class for constant outbursts and heinous acts against students, teachers and even class pets—as the science class hamster found out. One day, Lily didn't come back to school. Jimmy hadn't seen her since.

When he passed by on his way to town, he couldn't help but notice the farm and farmhouse had both deteriorated— he wasn't even sure they still lived there. Whispers around town blamed every missing person on Lily—although they never proved anything. His parents had warned him to stay away from there.

But, on this summer night, the neglected, overgrown corn stalks and tall grass provided cover for the two curious teens. They were hiding in the soft blades from the bright, lunar orb. The term, *knee-high-by-July* went out the door when the farmer hadn't plowed the crop from the year before. The boys, Jimmy and Robbie, were flat on their stomachs, slithering through the unkept lawn in attempt to spy on the farmer's mysterious daughter. Rumors among the younger crowd of the nearest town was that Old Man Dale's daughter was a dark-haired siren with sun-kissed skin and a wild side.

The older folks gossiped that any boy that approached Lily was sure to be seduced and never heard from again. Jimmy and Robbie hoped for seduction and paid no mind to the rest of the tales. They were a pair of clumsy, hormonal goofballs. They hoped for a peek, a silhouette, maybe even a kiss–if they were lucky–from the sweet lips of the lovely Lily.

Army style crawling on their bellies, side to side, the boys pushed each other backward as they competed for the first glimpse of her. Jimmy braced himself with one hand on the handle of an old wheel barrel while he used his other hand to wipe mud from a water-leaking hose onto Robbie's mouth and claimed it was pig manure.

He laughed as Robbie twisted his freckled face away in disgust and quickly pawed at his face to get it off, so he didn't see what Jimmy did next. Jimmy's laughter caught in his throat. Motion on the second floor, a quick shadow from the left to the right, crossed the dimly lit window.

While his rival wiped his face and spit mud into the grass, Jimmy stayed fixated on the upper window. He saw motion again, left to right, and then the shadow stopped. The room brightened slightly, and Jimmy could see the curvaceous form of a slender female clad in a long, white nightgown.

She stood in front of a tall floor mirror and lifted her long, dark hair up into a ponytail and then let it drop down to below her mid-back. Jimmy was mesmerized. He didn't even hear Robbie the first time he swooned at what he was also seeing.

Robbie said, in a voice that may have been a little too loud, "Fantastic!"

Jimmy didn't remove his eyes from her as he replied dreamily, "Yes."

Just then, a petite, black cat jumped up on the decaying wheel barrel as if to see what the boys were up to, effectively startling them both. Robbie picked up a small stick and threw it at the cat. The curious feline flinched when the stick bounced off its chest and it jumped down to inspect the piece of wood on the ground. When the boys looked back to the window, the girl was gone. They both sighed in disappointment.

Robbie asked, "Welp, wanna come back tomorrow night?"

Jimmy pursed his lips to the side.

The pair was about to crawl back to the decaying corn field where they could stand and walk home when they heard a door slam.

They held still and quiet as they watched the girl softly trot down the porch steps and turn to her right; away from them and onto the path, through the corn stalks leading out to the large red barn. Her gown left a luminescent illusion of a trail in the moonlight like a comet.

Both boys shot to their feet. Jimmy brushed off the grass from his blue flannel shirt. Robbie shoved Jimmy backward. Jimmy fell over the wheel barrel–his breath was knocked out of him for a moment. He raised his head and saw Robbie laughing and running in Lily's direction.

Jimmy winced at the small gash on the back of his right hand, near his wrist bone, "That's gonna leave a mark," he said aloud.

He moved his legs from the wheel barrel and rolled over onto his hands and knees. When he got to his feet, Lily was already in the barn and Robbie had slowed down from a sprint to a winded walk.

Jimmy looked up at the night sky, the gigantic harvest moon had climbed higher in the night sky and looked more like a normal full moon now and still quite bright. There was enough light to see where he was going and where Lily and Robbie had gone before him.

Alone in the dark, he wasn't so confident anymore. His hand was bleeding. He had removed his blue flannel and wrapped it around his wound. His white t-shirt gleamed in the effulgence, just as Lily's gown, but Jimmy's t-shirt had a smear of fresh blood across his shoulder where he'd removed the over-shirt carelessly.

Also, he now noticed that his ankle hurt and there was a scratch across his back that pained when his shirt brushed against it. He debated on not entering the barn. This wasn't his best first impression for Lily to see him in this condition. But, he certainly wasn't going to allow Robbie to charm her uninterrupted.

Jimmy decided he would go in and throw off Robbie's attempt at swooning the farmer's daughter; he reckoned Robbie had it coming.

Jimmy pushed light into the barn with the heavy wooden door. When it shut behind him he realized it wasn't pitch black. The roof had holes in it and the bright beams cut through the room like spears thrown into the dirt floor.

Jimmy tried to be quiet as he moved slowly through the barn. The smell was overwhelming. It was a mixture of moldy hay, the spectral scent of pigs and horses long gone, and…something else he couldn't quite pin-point.

The barn was long and narrow and made up of two parallel rooms that were separated by one large door in the middle that slid open, rather than swung.

At first, everything was silent. Then, as Jimmy turned left and stepped into the second room, he looked to his right and saw Lily standing at the far end of the stretched-out room with her back to Robbie, who was standing close enough to touch her.

Jimmy watched as Robbie reached out to put his hand on Lily's arm when she suddenly spun around, her dark hair spread out in the air and landed across her back. Her face was wild and frightening even. Her mouth was not a pretty, painted smile but that of a shrieking banshee!

Her teeth bared and displayed like a rabid dog. Her eyes were fiery and lit up with what Jimmy could only describe as anger, hunger, or need. She reached out for Robbie with one hand and he stumbled backward and fell.

Lily seized the opportunity to drop down onto her gown-clad knees over him. In her hand she gripped a butcher knife. She brought the knife down and when she raised it up again, it was covered in blood… Robbie's blood! Robbie was screaming as the knife released his life force into the night air. His hands flailed, but only managed to get in the way of the blade once.

Jimmy was frozen as Robbie's screams turned into gurgling and then silence. Lily continued her attack for a few more stabs after Robbie was gone. She sat back on her ankles. Her gown was a splattered pattern of dots, blobs, and streaks. She sat quiet for a moment, her chest slowing as she collected her breath. She transferred the steel blade from one hand to the other and flexed her crimson fingers.

Jimmy stared in slack-jawed horror as she watched her hand. She closed her fingers and smiled as they stuck together when she pulled them apart: closed, open, closed, open; stick, stick, stick.

She was gazing at her drying mess in a trance-like state, her hand splayed in front of her face, when she must have noticed she wasn't alone. Her eyes jumped quickly to Jimmy. Her faded smile returned into a wicked grin. She struggled to get up, her long gown was trapped beneath her feet.

Jimmy felt paralyzed. In shock, his feet wouldn't budge. He felt sick, he might even be ill. But, even to vomit would require moving and Jimmy just couldn't.

Suddenly, there was a voice; distant, male. It was the farmer! Jimmy realized the old man was calling for his daughter.

Lily was back on her feet and charging his way. The farmer's disembodied voice in the night was enough to snap Jimmy out of his trance. He turned on his heel, pain shot through his injured ankle into his calf, he didn't care. He ran as fast as he could, not looking back.

He knew she was quick behind him, blade tearing at his sweat-soaked t-shirt. He swore he could feel the tip of her blade on his back as he ran through the corn stalks, all the way home, and for months thereafter; constantly looking over his shoulder.

Not Jimmy, nor anyone ever saw Lily, nor the farmer, again after that night. Police never found Robbie's body either, despite canine accompanied police hunts and state wide missing person searches.

Chapter One

"You're sure your friend is coming?" Ben asked his girlfriend Sarah from his cell phone.

"Yes, I'm sure. She's coming with me. She's already packed," she reassured him as she twisted her blond hair up into a messy bun.

"Okay, because if I bring Mark on this camping trip and she doesn't come with you, we will be stuck with him the whole week, just the three of us...the whole week," he threatened playfully.

"Whatever, we would pick up a hitchhiker if that happened," she laughed, "But no, that's not going to happen. I didn't drive all the way down here for nothing. We haven't seen each other in two years. Of course, she's coming."

"Great! This is going to be one heck of a blind date!" he exclaimed.

"Going to the show is a blind date. Going to a cabin and finding out you're going to spend the week with someone you've never met—well, I don't know what to call that," she laughed. "I told her she would have a good time and there would be guys around the campsite so, technically, I didn't lie. She will get there and maybe even fall for Mark and she won't even know it's a set-up," she promised.

"Fine," he relaxed, "just meet us at that one truck stop we

agreed upon."

"Okay, you're sure the car will be alright to leave with that Eddie guy?" she worried.

"Yes. It'll be tight, but it'll be fine. I want us all to ride together and, besides, I don't want to pay for gas for two cars," he said.

"Fine, we'll see you there in a couple of hours. I love you," she fare-welled.

"Love you, too."

~*~

Chapter Two

"This is a set-up, isn't it?" Anna accused her longtime friend.

"What?" Sarah acted innocently, "Why would you say that?"

Anna cocked her head, "Because you said you were meeting your boyfriend in that car over there and there are two guys in there," she pointed out.

Sarah smiled, "Well, here's the thing, we needed another person to help pay and Ben's friend paid for half the cabin but he didn't want to be a third wheel. We can't afford the cabin by ourselves so, please?" her eyes fluttering, "For old time's sake?"

Anna pursed her lips. If she hadn't just sat for two hours and really, really needed this vacation, she would have found a way home. But, she needed to get away from everything. Just because there would be some guy there didn't mean she had to hang out with him. It would be a big campground. She would make the best of it.

"Yeah, well, I'm about to bust," Anna said and went into the truck stop.

~*~

Ben and Mark got out of their car and Ben and Sarah hugged and kissed as lovers do when they haven't seen each other in a week. Mark gave them some privacy and went into the truck stop men's room. He heard the women's restroom door open as the men's door closed behind him.

When he came out of the bathroom, he noticed the small, round, denim-clad backside of a girl bent over and wondered what the rest of her looked like. He moved to the rack of postcards and glanced over. She glimpsed his way. When her shoulder-length chestnut hair moved from her face, his breath caught in his lungs. She was certainly attractive with her glossed lips and button nose, but her lined eyes and long lashes made his insides tighten.

Mark wanted to introduce himself, but he had no words. Instead, he turned into an aisle and pulled two bags of snacks that he didn't even know what they were off the wall. He looked back to see if she was still there. She had moved around the display case to face the aisle. She looked up at him and he panicked. He turned and ran into a rack of phone chargers. She smiled and looked back down at the blown-glass figurines.

Mark went to the coolers. He opened the cooler door and grabbed two bottles of water. He stood in the chilled air for a moment. He mumbled under his breath to himself, "What's wrong with you?"

When he stepped away from the coolers and faced the aisle once more, she was gone. He looked left and right but didn't see her. A sadly he realized he'd missed his opportunity.

Mark went to get in line to pay for his things. His hands were full, and he wasn't even sure what he was buying. He didn't care either. He stood behind a large bald man in black leather buying nacho chips and beer. He noticed that two young pre-teen girls come up behind him with their hands full of sour candy and fountain drinks.

He swept the store with his eyes once again in hopes to see her. She was gone. Suddenly, the sound of giggling girls behind him, the beeping of register buttons being poked, and background muzak was interrupted by a rumbling noise behind him. It sounded as though someone had eaten something that didn't agree with them.

Mark didn't even want to look back. The sound quickly escalated to the expulsion of gas that almost didn't even sound real. He was ready to hold his breath if it came to that. The sound was beginning to attract attention, and, for some reason, the attention was all on him.

He glanced behind him and the young girls had backed up from him and were giving him crazy eyes. As his chin reached his shoulder, he realized the splatter-sputter sound was coming from behind him; more to the point, from his back pocket. And it was getting louder.

When Mark turned his head to the front, he saw that the chestnut-haired beauty had been in line in front of the large bald man, tucked in neatly from his view. But, now, she was leaning into position with everyone else twisting to see who was suffering from the worst case of gas imaginable.

His hands were full. He couldn't reach his pocket to shut off his cell phone or throw it into another dimension even. He wanted to crawl into a hole. He did the only thing he could do, he calmly put his snacks and water down on a nearby counter and left to knock his friend out.

When Mark reached the car, he saw Ben and Sarah barely holding it together. Mark was sure the look on his own face was enough to tell that he was angry.

Mark and Ben have been good friends since Middle School. Ben even lived with Mark for the month he and Sarah were on a break. He knew Ben had a jocular wit and was somewhat a prankster. One of the reasons Ben and Sarah had a sometimes-rocky relationship was due to his prank-and-tape sense of humor.

Ben once switched Sarah's shampoo with pink hair dye, and, while it didn't dye her hair too much, it did streak her hands for a while. Mark knew for sure that Ben must've changed his cell phone's ringtone while he slept on their way there.

As Mark approached the two, he had no idea what to even say.

"What's the matter, my guy? Tummy got a rumbly?" Ben was swirling his hand over his stomach.

"Why would you do that to me?!" Mark's raised voice was tempered by his equal need for privacy.

Ben laughed and pretended to be offended, "What so ever do you mean?"

Mark slammed, "You're a real dick, you know that?"

Ben pouted his lower lip, "Who cares anyway? It's a truck stop. AND, I didn't even tape it to share with the public."

Mark pinched the bridge of his nose for focus and said, "No, there was a girl in there. I was going to approach her when…" he trailed off.

Ben laughed harder, "So, what, you were standing there in front of this girl, about to ask for her number when your arse went off?"

Mark narrowed his eyes and tilted his head, "No, I couldn't find her. Then, when my phone went off, she looked and that's when I saw that she was in line."

Sarah broke into the conversation, "Wait, was she pretty?"

Mark smirked, "Yes, why else would I be so upset?"

Sarah smiled, "How pretty?"

Mark furrowed his brow, "Drop-dead, knock-out, gorgeous-pretty."

Sarah asked, "Was she wearing skinny jeans and a white shirt that fell over her shoulder?"

Mark's eyes widened, "Yeah, why?"

"Because she's coming out of the truck stop now," Sarah informed.

Mark heard the door chime and quickly spun his attention away from the door. He quietly urged, "Don't look at her! She'll see me!"

Sarah grinned out of one side of her mouth, "Oh no, she's turning this way."

Mark shook his head tightly, "Don't get her attention. Let's just get in the car and go."

Sarah said, "She's coming this way, man. Maybe we should see if she needs a ride?"

Mark's eyes were like saucers, "Don't you dare! Let's go! Get in!"

Sarah laughed as she walked past Mark toward the girl. She swung her arm over the girl's shoulder and brought her around to face Mark, "Mark, Ben, this is my good friend, Anna. She's our number four."

Mark smiled politely at Anna and the two girls walked to the car and slid into their seats. Mark looked at Ben with tightly-clenched lips and large eyes. He took a deep breath and slowly shook his head.

Ben was attempting to hold in his laughter, but it escaped through his nose in a snort.

He put his hand on Mark's shoulder, "I didn't know, man."

Mark shrugged off Ben's hand and went to the car and got in quietly. He could hear Ben trail off, "I'm sorry, man," through muffled giggles.

Mark slipped into the back seat behind Ben. The small compact car's trunk wasn't large enough for everyone's luggage so one carry-on sized suitcase had to be put into the back seat. This made for little room for Mark and Anna.

Ben was pulling onto the highway when Mark found his voice.

"Hi, I'm Mark," he held out his hand.

Anna smiled at his hand and teased, "Are you contagious?"

Mark swayed his head away from her and looked down with a smile on his face, "Ben!" he called out.

Ben looked at Mark through the rearview mirror, "Yeah?"

Mark said, "Help me out here, man. What did you do to my phone?"

Ben's green eyes were unapologetic, "I have no idea to what you are referring, my friend."

Mark dipped his head and gave Ben a raised-brow look of *'c'mon, man'*.

Ben laughed, "Okay, fine. Yes, Anna, I rigged Mark's phone to drop a major bomb and then I called him while he was in line at the truck stop. It was me. I am the phantom phone farter. I am sorry."

Sarah shook her head from her front passenger seat.

"Thank you, finally," Mark's chest felt lighter.

Anna's laugh made Mark happy. She had a great laugh.

Anna said, "I believe you. My little brother had that same ringtone about two years ago. He thought it was the funniest thing in the world until he got detention and had to spend two Saturdays in Study Hall."

Mark raised his eyebrows in supportive agreement.

Anna pointed at his pocket and said, "I'd change your ringtone soon though if I were you."

Mark smiled and agreed as he clicked his way to his default ringtone and then set it to vibrate only.

All four windows were down. It was 77° now that the sun was setting, and the view was spectacular. A rushing river of green grass parted by perfectly smooth pavement was gauged by a harmonious onslaught of mile markers and road signs.

Mark and Anna had scooted close to each other and leaned into one another in attempt to hold any resemblance of a conversation. The wind blowing into the car howled over them. Anna kept one hand around her hair to keep it out of her mouth. She wished she'd remembered her hair tie or a head band.

They talked like this for nearly two hours. Anna was drawn to Mark's light blue eyes and how they contrasted with his dark hair. He couldn't be more than a year older than she and only a foot taller. His smile was shy and inviting. He had remarkably long eye lashes. Even though the wind howled and made it hard to hear, she didn't mind just staring at him and nodding.

He wore a black hooded sweatshirt that had white letters going down his left sleeve. Anna couldn't read it as she was on his right. He had an athletic build. He wore a black rubber wristband on his right wrist and plucked at it with his thumb. Anna assumed it was from a concert he'd gone to recently, but that was just a guess. He wore a black canvas banded watch on his left. She saw it when he pulled his sleeves up.

Since she had first seen him in the truck stop, he'd run his fingers through the top of his hair three times. His hair parted down the middle and fell in a feathered pattern. Anna tried to keep her eyes on him, but she couldn't concentrate. Especially when he locked eyes with her. He was having an effect on her but the way he fidgeted, she could tell he was getting to him as well. She liked it.

Time passed, the highway narrowed, and the moon pushed the sun away. Anna wasn't accustomed to seeing the country star-scape–twinkling as far as the eye could see. There was a harvest moon climbing high above. The gigantic orb hung over them like a spotlight and the stars around it cowered out of sight.

Anna was in Heaven. The windows were now half-mast, the noise was down to a low roar, the air smelled sweet and Mark was an unexpected perk. She could see him out of the corner of her eye as he covertly stole glances her way. She liked that he wasn't very good at hiding his attraction. He seemed like a guy capable of playing hard-to-get but that he wasn't about games or pretending.

Anna was tired of playing games. As a bartender, she'd seen her fair share of pick-up lines and head games, both directed at her and her customers–male and female alike.

She felt confident she could spot a fake pretty easy and Mark seemed like the real deal. That quality was quite rare in her experience.

Anna stared off out the window for a moment and wondered to herself, 'What am I doing? So much uncertainty and I'm not even looking for anyone right now.'

Mark's genuine nature suddenly seemed intimidating. When she looked at him, she saw the long haul. And that was scary. Her life was simple. She had a small simple apartment. She had a simple job with late hours and no one to answer to.

On the other hand, she could be reading him completely wrong. He may be a classic mind game genius and just really good at hiding it. If that's the case, she would still be interested in getting close to him this week, but not too close.

Anna decided to stop over-thinking things. She would enjoy the summer, the campground atmosphere, the nights sitting around a crackling bonfire, roasting marshmallows.

She imagined four folding chairs encircled around a pit of gathered firewood, Ben poking it with dry timber while Sarah skewered spongy confection onto overpriced roasting forks purchased at the campground gift shop.

She imagined volleyball on the beach, grilling corn in tin foil and setting hot dogs on fire over the fire pit. She let her mind wander to paddle boating and especially horse back riding. The thought of Mark riding a brown and white spotted horse next to her, looking over at her and smiling as his denim-clad hips swayed side-to-side made her heart race.

She imagined him walking with her in the dark to the camp showers after an afternoon at the pool and dinner where she impressed them with her special roasted potato bombs she made from spuds and leftovers.

They'd take separate showers but, on the way back, it would start to rain, and they'd have to jog back and dive into his tent, laughing. The pelting rain would serenade them in a romantic lullaby. They would towel dry their hair and his lips would be wet. The lantern's glow would glisten off the left side of his face as his playful smile loosened into need.

His light crystalline eyes would realize the moment was changing and he would glance at her own lips like a reflex. She was sure it would only take a moment alone, one kiss and, like a Pit Bull off his chain, he would be unstoppable. She had hoped so anyway.

For now, she would sit next to him, enjoy what time they would be given as their legs occasionally bumped into each other 'accidentally'. She knew what it all meant. Or, maybe it was all in her mind. She woke and realized she'd been dreaming.

She twisted two fingers into the corners of her eyes softly to check for Sandman's Glue as she called it. It was what weighed down her eyelids at work at one o'clock in the morning. She straightened her back and peeked at Mark. His head was resting against the window, his lips parted slightly as his breathing was slow and peaceful.

When Anna moved, Mark stirred. He squeezed his eyes tight like he woke to a headache. He opened his eyes and looked over at her. She smiled back.

She looked out the window at the enchanted moon and then down at the blurry road and realized they weren't moving very straight anymore. They were drifting off to the left, closer to the tall wall of ripened corn stalks. She leaned up to look into the front seat. Sarah's head was laid against the headrest and she was asleep. She looked at Ben through the rearview mirror and realized, he too, was asleep! Mark must have noticed it at the same time as she did because he shouted, "Wake up!"

Ben jolted in his seat and gripped the steering wheel, but it was too late. They were already in a spin. Ben pulled the wheel back and forth in a desperate attempt to gain control but to no avail. The car swung to the left and right and the passengers could only hold on and go along for the ride. What seemed like minutes took only seconds as they bounced off a medium sized rock and landed twenty feet into the rows of tall corn stalks.

Chapter Three

"Jackass!" Mark yelled at Ben for falling asleep at the wheel. Ben wiped his eyes and down his face as the four of them stood around the front passenger side flat tire. Thankfully, they were mostly just shaken up. Mark's arm hurt and would probably be sore tomorrow. Anna's cheek had a slight scratch and her jeans were torn above the knee where something had gone through and gouged her skin. Both girls were shaking as if it were winter.

Mark went to the back as Ben popped the trunk and moved the luggage around. He pulled the spare tire out of a hidden compartment and it bounced on the ground. Mark watched as he rolled it to the side of the rear quarter panel and leaned it against the car and searched for the jack and tire iron. Ben leaned his head around the side of the open trunk lid and asked Sarah politely, "Hun? Where is the jack and tire iron?"

Everyone looked Ben's way. Sarah was hugging herself as she walked back to where he stood.

"You know I had that in my car because I had to travel to Michigan last week," she reminded him.

"Yeah," he seemed to struggle to maintain order in his voice, "but where is it now?"

She looked around the trunk floor, "Didn't you remember to transfer it to your car at the truck stop when you transferred the luggage?"

Mark took Anna around the front of the car and turned her face into the beam of the headlights and she closed her eyes to the light. He examined her scraped cheek. "Are you okay?" he asked with a note of concern in his voice. She let him look at her cheek and said, "Actually, my leg hurts worse but I'm fine."

He looked down at her tattered denim and stooped for a better view, "Oh yeah, that may need some attention. I don't think we have anything like first aid in the car though."

Behind the car, Ben slammed the trunk lid shut and said matter-of-factly, "Well, we're screwed."

Mark stood up and went back to Ben and asked, "What do you mean?"

Ben put his hand to his face and rubbed up his forehead and acted like it didn't matter, "Because, we just don't have any way of going anywhere, that's all."

Mark asked with forced patience, "Why not?"

Ben seemed to hold onto his own patience by a thread, "Because I didn't load the jack or the tire iron into the trunk when we dropped her car off with Eddie!"

Mark was a problem solver, but he was at a loss. After wasted moments of pacing and profanities, they all agreed they would stick together, find a house nearby and ask for help.

Ben tested the engine by starting it and shutting it off. They were all thankful that it was still able to run once they could get the tire changed. Ben locked the doors since they were leaving their luggage behind. With minimal supplies, they set off, on foot, to find a neighbor. There was only one house visible as far as the eye could see in any direction. It was massive. There were two visible stories plus attic and basement. A farmhouse set way back from the road and a barn surrounded by corn stalks.

The driveway was long and lined with rows of tall corn. Sarah held onto Ben as they walked along the gravel path. Mark and Anna brought up the rear. Anna wanted to take Mark's hand sheerly out of comfort but refrained. She didn't want to assume he would be okay with it and that was a scarier thought than any old farmhouse. Just as they passed a short, flat, tree stump, a black barn cat jumped up onto it.

Mark was startled and stumbled into her, almost sending them both to the ground. He apologized but sounded annoyed, "Stupid cat!"

Anna smiled despite his being upset, it was just funny. Ben and Sarah were far enough ahead that they didn't even notice. When they were all four on the wraparound porch, they noticed that there was only one light on and it was on the second floor. Ben knocked but no one came. The guys walked around the house but returned shaking their heads. It seemed no one was home.

Anna opened the screen door and turned the door knob, it creaked open. The guys rejoined them, and Ben led them in, then Mark, then the girls. Ben called out to see if anyone would answer but no one did. Sarah caught up with Ben and hung onto his forearm. Like Shaggy and Scooby, left to partner, Mark and Anna chose to check out the second floor. Ben and Sarah stayed on the first floor and headed off to the kitchen.

Anna stayed behind Mark as they climbed the old weathered stairs. Mark's eyes were straight forward, wide and ready for anything, Anna's eyes were uncontrollably focused on Mark's tight rear end. She recalled her fevered dream of Mark riding that horse, bouncing and rocking.

Mesmerizing, she thought. As they reached the top, she shook off her trance. She would need to get a hold of herself if she were going to keep from embarrassing herself. The hallway that stretched out in front of them was long and dark. Mark used the flashlight on his cell phone to light the way. He stopped and checked his reception and said, "Well, it looks like we have no reception out here."

Anna put her hand in her back pocket, "Crap. My phone must be in the car. I don't think I'd have any better luck getting out either."

The hardwood floor was softened slightly by a carpeted runner that ran the length of the hallway in front of them. There were three round side-tables, one beside each of the three doors in the out-stretched corridor and one more door at the very end of the hallway on the left. On each table sat a candle and beside the first candle was a pack of matches.

Mark lit all three candles. Anna followed him closely, feeling uneasy. They went back to the first room on their right. Mark turned the knob and it was unlocked. He glanced back at her as the door cracked open loudly as though the paint tried to seal it forever.

Inside was a large, white canopy bed. Lace curtains reached the hardwood floor. On the bedside table was an oil lantern. There was a white dresser and matching vanity. Across the room sat a wood-framed full-length cheval mirror.

It seemed to be a girl's bedroom, unused for some time. Mark grabbed the lantern, lit it, and carried it with him back into the hallway. He slipped his cell phone into his back pocket to preserve the battery.

They both had a light source as she carried the lit candle. The room was empty other than the furniture. They wanted to keep exploring so they went toward the next room. As the light followed him out, she saw, out of the corner of her eye, in the full-length mirror, a glimpse of a man standing behind her. She felt as though the wind had been knocked out of her. Fear shot through her body and she jerked her head back to the reflection but there was no one. She spun around to where the man would be standing but she was alone. Alone! She didn't want to be alone in that room.

Trick of the mind? She thought, *creepy old farmhouse getting to her? Possibly.* But, for a figment of her imagination, she had seen him quite detailed. He had worn blue overalls and a red, long sleeved, flannel shirt. She looked around the room again for something blue and red that she could have mistaken for a man but as Mark's light ran from the room, she saw no such thing. She caught up with him. Back in the hallway, there were three doors to go, two on the left and one on the right.

Mark suggested, "How about you check the one on the left and I'll check the one on the right?"

She nodded, "'Kay," and hesitantly opened the heavy door. She wanted to stay with him, but she brushed it off. He would be in the next room if she yelled and she didn't want to look like a baby. He gave her the lit lantern and exchanged it for her candle. He went down the hall to the last door on the right. He stopped, and they took one last look at each other and then he went in.

She pushed the heavy door open and peered in. She put the lantern on the bedside table. The room brightened somewhat. She did a complete 360° and visually swept the perimeter. No large mirrors, she was relieved. This room also seemed untouched for quite some time. A king-sized bed dressed in chenille commanded attention, centered and covered in shammied pillows. There was a small, brown teddy bear resting in front of the bedding.

The dresser was long instead of tall. There was nothing on it but a set of three vintage looking dolls in Victorian style dresses. She went to the window and looked out at the grounds below. There was a fantastic view of the crops and the barn. *They should check the barn for a jack and tire iron,* she thought.

From behind her she heard a whisper; nothing discernible, just a light, inaudible voice in the dark. She turned on her heel, but the room was empty except for the three menacing dolls. She began to cross the room to check them in further detail.

Mark had left his door open as he surveyed the room. It was empty. He assumed this must have been the guest wing. The bed was only a full size, smaller and less elaborate than the one in the first room they'd inspected. It wore a blue and white comforter and had matching curtains.

He saw another lantern perched on the night stand beside the bed. He used his candle to light the lantern and blew out the candle. The lantern was brighter with a larger footprint.

He crossed the room and the floor creaked with every step. As he walked beyond the foot of the bed, one of the boards gave in and his foot went through. He yelped as the floor swallowed his leg up to his knee. He caught the lantern from hitting the hardwood floor and set it down next to him. His leg burned, and his heart pounded.

~*~

When Anna heard Mark yell, she turned from the dolls to face the door, but it was shut. Her chest fell. She didn't remember closing the door, "What is going on here?" she asked herself aloud.

She traversed the room and turned her back to the dolls to twist the knob, but it didn't open. She tried again, the lock wouldn't release. She heard a whisper, a disembodied voice in the dark, but was too afraid to look. She stifled the rising panic in her entire body. Nothing could possibly be behind her. She knew that rationally. But, irrationally, she knew she wasn't alone in that room.

~*~

Mark tugged at his foot but, somehow, his shoe was stuck in the hole. He sat, more aggravated than anything else. The splintered wood had scraped his skin and it burned above his ankle. He moved his foot side to side and in a circle in attempt to free himself and rolled his eyes in frustration when it didn't work. "C'mon," he sighed in complaint.

He looked around the room for something he could use. As his eyes searched, he glanced by the bed and saw two tiny amber lights underneath. He flinched, 'Eyes?' he asked himself. He squinted to comprehend what he was seeing. He tried to mentally dismiss it as his imagination, but they were unwavering.

They stared at him, flickering and fixed upon him. He grew uncomfortable. "Another cat," he told himself, "What's it doing under the bed?" He twisted at his foot, but his shoe kept him at bay. He kept his gaze on the two beady lights and, in his mind, tried to explain the lights as a trick of the low light, a reflection from his lantern. *Probably buttons or beads,* he rationed. He began to relax until they moved, in unison, closer.

His brow furrowed as he focused on the moving beams and tried to explain them away. But they moved again, slowly closer. He heard a vibrating, growl-hiss and was sure, "Cat! Just great!" he said, half relieved, half annoyed; he hated cats.

He put one hand inside the hole and felt for his laces. He would have to take his shoe off to get his foot out. Suddenly, as he pulled on his laces, he felt fur brush against the back of his hand and he yanked his hand up out of the hole. He looked again under the bed, but the two eyes had multiplied to four.

"What the…?"

~*~

Anna twisted and pulled, twisted hard and pulled harder. The door wouldn't budge. She kept her eyes to the front, too unwilling to admit that she was afraid to turn around. She imagined the dolls whispering to each other like mean children did when they told secrets about classmates; giggling and pointing.

She also envisioned them walking slowly toward her like tiny zombies, wobbling to and fro. Tiny teeth snapping shut dramatically and wielding butcher knives like something straight out of 1968's Barbarella movie.

She hit her fist against the heavy wood. *Maybe,* she thought, *someone would hear her and come help her.* She tried to stay calm and not completely lose it. It wasn't easy, and she was losing the battle with her nerves. Just then, the whisper grew a little louder, a little closer, a little clearer. She heard, "You can have the girl, but I want the boy."

She had held onto her sanity long enough. Like the Fates holding scissors to the thin thread of her composure, it snapped. She double-fisted the door and yelled for Mark desperately.

Something more than fear, more than she'd ever experienced before, raced through her body. She was trapped in the room with someone or something and she could feel its cold breath on the nape of her neck just as her lantern went out.

~*~

Chapter Four

Mark fought with the floorboard to give him back his leg. He fought with himself to keep control as the darkness developed two more eyes and advanced, growling and hissing. They spat at him as they taunted him.

Just then, he heard Anna beating on a door and calling his name. She sounded frantic. He fought harder to get free. He had to get to her. He suddenly felt very protective of her and she sounded like she may be in trouble. The fear in her voice mirrored what he was feeling. With the irrational things going on in this room, he didn't want to imagine what might be terrifying her in the next.

He put his hand back in the hole and, as he found his shoe lace, he felt a tail swipe his knuckles again. He jumped and jerked his hand up but not all the way out. He found the laces again and pulled them loose. "Yes!" he said with satisfaction.

He stuck his finger under the laces to open the mouth of his shoe. Another pair of amber eyes opened in the inky blackness under the bed. Nothing was making sense anymore. *Where were the cats coming from? What was going on here?*

Mark was prying at his foot to come out of his shoe when he realized the hissing had stopped. He stretched his neck over his left shoulder to see if the eyes were gone, they were. Relief washed over him. He could finally begin to pretend none of it had happened.

Just then, in the far corner, across the room, a guttural sound penetrated the side of the room that the light didn't reach. It sounded like a cat but larger and mixed with what Mark hallucinated as human; female.

Low, in the corner, eyes unlike the ones beneath the bed, popped open. Iridescent, yellow and more human than cat. The eyes stared at him and he couldn't look away. The disembodied eyes rose as though they were attached to something and that something was standing up.

The intense eyes burned with anger and intent. Before Mark could blink, the eyes were rushing toward him!

Anna kicked the door. She could feel the presence of someone or something all around her. Where was Mark? Could he not hear her? She had heard him yelp, was he okay? She wanted to get to him. Just then, she heard a soft hiss in her ear and she closed her eyes. She prepared herself for whatever was about to happen to her when the door knob turned, popped open and light illuminated the empty room.

She yanked it all the way open and ran right into Sarah. She balanced herself and looked back at the door. She looked inside, and nothing was out of place. She scanned the room in disbelief and then turned away. "Where's Mark?" she practically shouted as she ran for the room he had gone into.

Ben and Sarah followed her into the room. They ran into each other to keep from piling up into Anna as she was stopped in the doorway. Mark had his arms up as though he was blocking an attack. He let his arms fall when they rushed in.

They all looked down at Mark with his foot stuck in the hole. Mark twisted his body to see them. Ben and Sarah burst into laughter. Anna was still too concerned for his safety and sober from her own ordeal to join in their hysterics but, as she looked at him and realized he was okay, she also realized how cute he was stuck in the floor. As relief washed over her, a laugh bubbled within her. She let it escape and he looked up at her and asked, "Great, now you too. Is anyone gonna help me?"

Anna knelt down and used Mark's lantern to see down inside the hole. Her hand was smaller, and her arm was thinner than his. She reached down and wriggled his shoe lace until his foot was free. She reached in and pulled his shoe out.

~*~

Mark took out his cell phone, clicked on the flashlight feature, and shined it down inside the hole, only emptiness and splintered wood. He shined the beam under the bed and there was nothing. He lit up the corner across the room, nothing. He turned off the flashlight and put his cell phone back into his pocket. He didn't want to waste battery; it was low already. The "No Network" sign was still all he got whenever he tried to use it.

Mark put his shoe back on and they all went back into the hallway. He wasn't normally one to admit his fear and he wasn't about to start now. He certainly didn't want to stand and talk in there.

He stepped out into the hallway and ran his fingers through his hair; something he did when he was nervous or uncomfortable.

"You okay?" Anna asked.

"Oh yeah, I'm fine," he reassured her with a light smile. He wondered if he was fooling anyone. He brushed his hands against each other to dust them off.

"I can't believe you fell in the floor. You were stuck in there the whole time," she shook her head.

"Yeah," he stepped closer to her, "I heard you screaming and pounding but I was really stuck. You had me worried," he admitted protectively.

Mark didn't want to admit that to himself either. His conversation with Anna in the car had only been about two hours long but, he couldn't deny their chemistry. They liked many of the same things, from food to TV shows. They even had nearly the same sense of religious and political beliefs, which was rare in his experience.

She's smart, intellectual, sensual, witty, beautiful, artistic and offered genuine heart, he admired. These were all things he wished he could find in someone to just be himself. But, he'd been burned too many times to let down his guard. She just made it so easy to let himself go and relax.

Anna didn't want to let him know how afraid she was, "I don't know how it happened," she said honestly, "but that door was not opening. How did you fall in the hole?" she smiled as she recalled the image of him stuck knee-deep in the floor.

"I just walked across the room," he said. He seemed uneasy or as though he didn't want to worry her about something, "I think that stupid cat got in here somehow though. Did you see one run out?"

"No, I didn't see any cat. Is everything okay?" She wondered if something had happened to him as well. There had been a cat outside that had scared them, but she hadn't seen any cats inside.

"Yeah, I'm fine. My leg is a little scratched up but it's all good."

Standing in the hallway, Sarah yawned, "Well, I think we should just sleep here and look for the jack and tire iron in the daylight. Maybe someone will come home in the morning and help us," she suggested.

Ben agreed, "Yeah, we can use these three bedrooms. Sarah and I can take this one," he indicated to the room with the three dolls. Anna was relieved. She wasn't in any hurry to go back into that room.

Ben continued, "And you guys can fight over the other two," he smiled devilishly, "Or… you guys can share *one* room," he instigated, waggling his eyebrows.

Mark and Anna looked at each other briefly and she blushed. Thankfully, red cheeks weren't visible in candlelight. Sarah thumped Ben on the arm, "Stop it, leave them alone." Ben laughed and pulled Sarah into the room with three whispering dolls.

"Well, which room do you want?" Anna asked.

"I'd actually rather not have the room with the hole in the floor, if that's okay with you."

"No, that's perfectly alright, I'll take it," she said relieved. She remembered the full-length mirror in the other room and cringed.

"Alright then, sweet dreams. Let me know if you need me," he said and walked down the hall to the mirror room. She tossed him the box of matches back and she watched him go but she really wanted him to stay. She didn't want to be alone in the hallway, so she went in and closed the door.

Chapter Five

Sarah went up to the dresser and touched the lace on the dolls' dresses. She pulled open one of the drawers and was pleased to find folded towels. She tossed one over her arm. Ben came up behind her and pressed himself into her. She smiled and turned to kiss him, "I saw a bathroom down the hall. I think I'm gonna go get cleaned up first," she smiled. She moved toward the door and turned back around, "Did you say something?" she asked.

"Nope, hurry up though." He was always so impatient. She went to the door and shrugged. She could have sworn she'd heard a whisper. She went out into the hall and down to the bathroom for a shower.

Sarah wasn't looking forward to a candlelit bath. She hoped there would, at least, be running water. The hallway was dark, and the floor creaked beneath her feet.

She reached the white wooden door and turned the antique door knob. The door cracked open as though age had sealed it long ago. Instead of cob webs and stale air, she was surprised to see light pour out. When she pushed open the door the farthest it would go, it hit against a rubber stopper on the wall inside.

She squinted slightly, partly from confusion. Was the electric working in parts of the house? They did see one light on when they first entered the house, but this was on the back side–not where they saw the light coming from before. Were the bulbs just burnt out in the other rooms? Sarah went in. The walls were bright yellow. Yellow painted paneling covered the lower four feet and from the paneling up was yellow wallpaper with tiny white flowers.

On the left, the counter and basin that was once white had yellowed now as though it were just trying to fit in. The room was long and somewhat narrow. There was a claw-foot bathtub against the back wall that filled end of the room, left to right. There was a pale-yellow curtain hanging from a curtain rod.

She closed the door behind her and checked herself in the mirror. Her eyeliner was smudged, and her white tank top was dirty. In the accident, she'd bruised her elbow. She bent it around to see it in the mirror. Just then, the lights flickered. In between moments of darkness, Sarah thought the room looked different. The reflected walls behind her looked decayed and the mirror went dark for just a second. The lights flickered back on and the room was bright, cheery even.

Sarah paused and looked around the room, but nothing looked out of the ordinary. The paint was not peeling off the walls. It even smelled pleasant; a sort of lavender meets mint. She shrugged off the event. She assumed the stress was getting to her. An accident, this creepy old house, being stranded–it was enough to put her on edge.

She pulled her straight blond hair up into a high, messy bun and unbuttoned her shorts. There was a soft, white rug under her feet, so she kicked off her sandals and let the fluffy rug fill the spaces between her toes. It felt good to get those sandals off. She undressed down to her undergarments, leaving her clothes on the rug and pulled the yellow curtain to the right.

It was remarkably clean for an old farmhouse; not what she expected at all. It was more like a bed and breakfast style bathroom. There was a small window high up on the wall and moonlight added a black-and-white aspect to the vibrant, shiny atmosphere.

She was disappointed to see there wasn't a shower head. She wasn't a fan of baths, "Dang. At least it's clean."

The water was not only running, but it was hot. "Nice," she said as she ran her hand under the stream.

She sat on the side of the tub as the water filled up. She pulled her cell phone from her denim shorts, but she had no reception, so she held it out at arm's length, took a selfie, and tossed it back onto her clothes. "I'll post that later when I get some bars," she planned.

After shedding the rest of her intimates, Sarah sunk down into the steaming bath. She wished she'd brought her new orchid scented foaming body wash in along with something clean to wear from her luggage. She'd figure that out in the morning, since she wouldn't need anything more than the towel for the night.

She soaked up to her shoulders and closed her eyes. *Even her bath at home wasn't this relaxing.* With the curtain pulled shut, the moonlight kept the space she occupied in a dim, pleasant balance.

At 5' 7", her legs were a little longer than the bathtub. Her knees broke the surface of the water as it was more comfortable to bend them.

With her eyes closed, she was unable to see the room flicker once again. All the color seeped down the walls and the paint peeled in decay. The cheery atmosphere bowed to the rot as the lights went out. Floor tiles broke, and some were missing altogether. Debris and filth collected in the corners.

Oblivious of the reality of the condition of the room, Sarah soaked in a mixture of sludge, slime and something unidentifiably jellied.

Sarah lay there, lost in her thoughts. Believing the room was how she'd imagined, steamy clean water soothing her stress away. She brought her hand up to her collarbone to scratch an itch. Her hand went back down under the muck. The itch persisted. She was irritated that her hair was tickling her shoulders.

Then, she remembered, she had pulled her hair up into a bun. She flicked whatever it was off at the same time she opened her eyes to see what it could be. When her eyes focused, she came eye-to-eye with a snarling and wicked face. Dark hair hung on either side of her vein-streaked face and was brushing against Sarah's shoulders.

The white-gowned demon-girl crouched over Sarah, and when Sarah screamed, the demon pushed her face under the muck. Sarah fought, thrashing side-to-side, to get up. She dug her manicured nails into the demon's soft grey flesh. It only laughed.

Then, as suddenly as it began, the demon-girl was gone. Sarah sat up, wiping her face and coughing the ooze from her lungs as she tried to catch her breath. She struggled to push the curtain to the left. The moon coming through the high window was the only light. The bright bulbs in the medicine cabinet were distinguished. Sarah tripped over the tub as she fought to get out of the disgusting liquid.

As she landed on the cold, cracked floor, she clutched the only thing that was real, her towel. She looked back at the bathtub to see the demon-girl's head resting on the side of the tub, smiling at her. Its hands clutched the porcelain. Its hair was matted. Its mouth and fingers were black.

Sarah stopped breathing as the demon-girl's head rolled along the edge of the bathtub as though it was just a head with no body. It made three rolls before it sunk back down into the ooze. Sarah scrambled back to her feet and wrapped the towel around her body.

She couldn't make sense of what she'd just went through, but she knew one thing, she and the others were getting out of here–even if they had to run to the next town. She grabbed her shorts and top as she got up and opened the door to the hallway.

She moved through the doorway. As she grabbed the doorknob to pull the door shut behind her, a grey arm shot out from the bathroom. Blackened fingers wrapped around Sarah's wrist and jerked her back inside. The bathroom door slammed shut.

~*~

Chapter Six

Ben flopped onto the bed, feeling anxious for Sarah to return. He paced the room, pulling open dresser drawers and looking out the window. He bent close to the three dolls. "Creepy," he said as he bopped one on the head with his finger.

He was getting sleepy. *She'd better hurry up if she's getting some of this,* Ben smiled. The bed looked small but comfortable. If he just rested his eyes for a minute…

As soon as his head hit the pillow, he heard a whispered voice. He raised his head and looked around the room but saw no one. He shrugged it off and put his head back down. A light whispering was fuzzy in his ears.

He grew aggravated. He propped himself up on his elbows and looked around the dark room. A confused look twisted his face. He waited long minutes and heard nothing more. He wanted Sarah to come back so that he could get it off his mind. Burying himself in his girlfriend would take away the creeps for sure.

Eventually, he grew heavy lidded and his body relaxed. He slipped backwards from his propped position and rested, once again, onto the comfy bed. And, once again, the whisper filled his head. Only this time it was a woman's voice and he clearly heard his name. He imagined long arms stretching up from either side of the pillow to wrap around his mouth.

He immediately sat up and stared down at the pillow. He

hesitantly leaned in onto his fingertips and put his ear to the delicately covered padding.

He waited and suddenly heard it louder, "Bennnjaminnn." He grabbed the pillow and threw it across the room. His heart pounded. He couldn't make sense of it. He wasn't a fearful person, but he didn't like being alone in this room. "What's taking her so long?" he said with agitation.

He got up and stood on the hardwood floor, barefoot. He stared at the pillow lying on the floor against the wall. He began to doubt the absurdity of it, but not enough to lie back down yet.

He looked at the dolls and felt the same creepy vibe he felt before. Only this time it was harder to shrug off. "Get a grip on yourself," he pep-talked himself. He went to the window and looked out over the entire crop. He saw the barn standing tall in the moonlight, also, the corn ready for harvest. Then, he saw Sarah. She was outside and running through the tall grass on a path to the barn. Confused, he said, "Sarah?" even though he knew she couldn't hear him, "Sarah!" he tapped on the glass.

He knew there was no way she could hear him from this distance but, somehow, she did. She stopped running, turned and stared at him, expressionless. He waved his hand slightly in front of the pane to keep her attention, but she turned and continued to run to the barn.

"Sarah!" he demanded, but she was gone, disappearing into the barn. He rushed to get his shoes on and left the room. He ran down the curved staircase and out the front door.

Chapter Seven

Mark lay in the canopy bed, feeling a little emasculated for taking the room with the girly bed, but he wasn't about to stay there with ghost cats under his bed in the other room.

It couldn't have been real, he thought. *But, it seemed so real. Maybe there's a gas leak here somewhere and I was hallucinating.*

The canopy's decorative upholstery was too much, in his opinion–it had to go. He stood and pulled on the fabric until it came loose and rolled it up like hand-muffs in the winter. He tossed it on a chair. "Much better," he nodded.

He wondered how Anna was doing in there. He felt guilty for not telling her about his experience and those amber eyes, glaring, darting, hissing, growling and snarling as they had crept closer to him. He shivered. He wanted to know if she would have an experience as he had. If she saw the cats, he would know he wasn't crazy.

But, more than that, he thought about how she was just one short hallway away from him. He hadn't admitted it to her, but, even in the short time they'd known each other, he knew he was falling for her. He wasn't sure how she felt about him, but the way she leaned into him in the car and how her eyes were warm, and welcoming told him she may feel the same.

He didn't know how to act around her or what to say. He had no idea what she was feeling, how she felt about him. When they were spooked in the stairway, coming upstairs, she'd stayed close to him and it made her seem small and trusting. He wanted to be her hero. He wanted to chase away her fears and hold her from the world's troubles. He stared up at the ceiling, his eyes focused in on a black spot in the center of the room. It helped him focus.

Mark wanted to go to her room and just be near her, talk to her and laugh with her. Cats or no cats, he wanted to go to her room. But, the thought of knocking on the door, standing there, staring at him–What would he even say?

The lantern was growing dimmer, the light waned as his eyelids grew heavy. His racing thoughts calmed, and his heartbeat slowed until he drifted off.

The room darkened as though he kept the lantern lit with his consciousness. As he fell into slumber, so did the light. The dot on the ceiling he had stared at, was only a spot, black and perfectly round. As the last moments of his awareness abated, the spot grew in size, but stayed spherical in shape.

Like adjusting the footprint of a flashlight, the spot doubled, tripled, quadrupled. The inky center became blurred and tendrils of black strands fell from it and clung to the ceiling above the blissfully unaware Mark.

The fibrous strands slithered out from the spot that became a hole–spidering out in every direction to cover the ceiling. As it continued down the walls, blocking out the moonlight from the window, blackened fingertips hung down from the hole, folded and pried it open.

The crown of a head, the source of the slithering fibers rooted from the head. A grey face streaked with dark veins followed next, straining against the diameter, widening as it came through.

The walls dripped with hair. The stringy threads left the wall and stretched across the divide, onto the headboard, over and around Mark's deep-sleeping body. The tendrils wrapped around his arms on both sides. Moving down, they enveloped his torso and then his legs.

A wicked grin formed across the cracked lips of the hovering witch as she forced her way from the hole. The hair she commanded was moving to cover her victim's face. Soon, he would be hers.

Chapter Eight

Anna carefully stepped around the hole that Mark had fallen into. She didn't want the same thing to happen to her and be stuck in the floor all night if no one heard her call for help. She smiled as she pictured his blushed cheeks and embarrassed expression.

She searched her pockets for a stick of gum she had been saving. She was getting hungry but wasn't about to go venturing to the kitchen alone. She chewed her gum and looked at the small bed, it would do. She wasn't even tired. She went to the dresser and pulled open the drawer. Folded handkerchiefs placed perfectly. She shut it and opened the second drawer, it was full of keys; small keys, large keys, oddly shaped keys and one that had a soda cap bent tightly around the base of it. She shut the drawer. She went to the bed and sat down. She wondered what time it was and if she was the only one feeling anxious.

She stuck her gum on the frame of the bed with the intention of throwing it away properly in the morning. She lay back and got comfortable. She closed her eyes but behind her lids, she saw only Mark. She wasn't going to sleep tonight, she realized. She thought about his smile when he laughed. His smooth-shaven cheeks and his strong jawline. His soft-looking, kissable lips. She wondered how good his lips felt. But what stood out the most were his crystal blue eyes in contrast to his dark hair. No matter how he looked at her, she grew warm.

She had an idea. She would go to his room and tell him she was too spooked to be in that room all alone. It wasn't too far from the truth anyway. This whole place was spooky.

She hadn't experienced anything yet in this room, but she was pretty sure the encounter she had in the room with the dolls wasn't uncommon for every room. It might just be a matter of time. She could be asleep, and a creepy whispering doll could be zombie-stepping into her room. No thanks. She had worked herself into enough of a creep-out to give her enough courage to go to his room. At least, when she told him she was afraid, she wouldn't be lying. She didn't want to think about the fear or strange goings-on in this old farmhouse. She wanted to think about him.

Her mind raced through the car ride they'd spent talking; how he moved. She liked how he turned his body toward her while they chatted. The way he ran his fingers through his hair when he searched for the right words excited her. His ability to laugh at himself was refreshing. He was actually quite witty, she reflected with a smile while recalling one of his jokes.

They had shared one blissfully frustrating two hours entwined in stimulating conversation. He was flirty but in a reserved, respectful manner. He grinned from the corner of his mouth when something crossed his mind, but he refrained to say. She could tell he was holding back.

She remembered how she desperately wanted to kiss him. The chemistry they shared was undeniable. But, what would the future hold for them? Would they fall in love over the next week at the campsite? She started getting excited about the upcoming week. She imagined over-the-shoulder glances at each other while horseback riding.

Gooey fingers while making smores by the bonfire together.

Her heart dropped and pounded in her chest at the thought of swimming in the lake. Sarah told her the campsite had two natural waterfalls and one was a bit secluded. Anna wished there was a working fan in her room as hot as it was getting.

She imagined she and Mark walking barefoot in the sand as he'd slide his hand in hers. They'd undress and leave their clothes on the rocks before floating around up to their necks. She imagined him standing in the deluge of the waterfall, his dark hair washing back, his blue eyes finding her as he wiped the water from his face. She wanted to swim up to him, run her hands up his tanned chest, around his neck and press her lips to his.

The room was absolutely smoldering. It was distracting her from her intoxicating dream. As she lay there picturing their lips together, tongues intertwined, bodies hungry, she thought she'd melt in reality. Reluctantly, she opened her eyes. She thought about opening the window for fresh air. It was so warm in the room that she briefly thought she smelled fire.

The scent of smoldering wood made the bonfire seem more realistic. She slipped down from the bed and stepped her teal painted toes onto the hardwood floor. Even the floor was warm. She soft padded over to the window, careful not to fall into Mark's hole, and looked out.

As her view was of the opposite side of the farmhouse than Ben and Sarah's room, she didn't see the barn, but the corn was just as tall and thick. She looked up at the night sky. She couldn't see the moon either from this side, but it was bright enough that she could see the silver light outlining the dark-bottomed clouds. *It might rain later tonight,* she thought to herself. *Maybe it'll cool it down in here*, she hoped.

When she looked down from the second story window, she thought she saw something walking through the rows of corn. From her aerial view she could see that it was moving fast. Whatever it was, it was about to exit the field into the yard. She pressed her forehead against the glass and looked down the bridge of her nose to see what it was. When it came out, she realized it was a cat. A tiger-striped tabby. She wondered if that was the cat to which Mark was referring.

It moved out of her line of sight. As she scanned the yard for anything else interesting enough to entertain her, she swallowed. Her throat was parched. She coughed. She couldn't stop coughing. She tried to open the window, but it was nailed shut. She backed away and noticed that the room was smoky.

Dark smoke had filled the ceiling and was choking her. She got down on her knees, close to the floor and crawled toward the door. It was getting hard to see. She put her hand down and felt her sandal. She caught the loops of both shoes and dragged them with her. She pulled her shirt up over her mouth and tried to breathe.

She didn't see any fire in the room, but the farmhouse had to be engulfed on the first floor, she rationed. That's why the floorboards were so warm.

She worried the hallway would be already consumed and she'd be opening the door to a flashover. She had no where else to go, she'd have to try. The door couldn't be far now.

She fought the urge to panic. The smoke was so thick she couldn't see where she was going anymore.

When she hit the wall, she reached up for the door knob but found the window sill instead. She realized she had somehow gotten turned around. She could barely see any light at all. She put her back to the window and faced where she knew the door was and crawled as fast as she could. She coughed as the effluvium engulfed her and struggled to find clean air.

When she reached the door, she weakly searched for the door knob. It wasn't there. It was the window sill again! Panic shot through her chest. She had no breath to scream. Her mind raced. There's only one window in this room. The door is on the opposite side. She'd been crawling in a straight line. It made no sense!

She kept her fingers on the window sill and faced where she knew the door was. She couldn't see anything, not even her hand in front of her face. Suddenly, she heard a wispy feminine voice. It said nothing audible, just a sigh as it grew louder as then it was gone. She heard it again as she strained to see where the tiny delicate sigh was coming from.

There, in front of her nose, a pin light was floating. She jolted backward and coughed. The pin light was the source of the wispy sigh. There were two pin lights, then three, then a whole lot of pin lights. They all sighed like spirits and fireflies. They lined up, one by one. She could see the first three, but the rest disappeared into the smoke.

Anna forced herself to let go of the window sill and crawl toward the lights. As she assumed, the further she crawled, the next pin light would appear. She heard the wisps sigh in her ear as they whizzed past her to extend her path at the front of the line. Her eyes watered, her nose ran, and her throat burned. The house must surely be consumed.

She wondered why she heard no screams, no sirens. The pin lights came to an end. She reached up and felt for the door knob. It was there! Oh, thank Heaven, the knob was in her hand. She thought for sure it would burn her hand as flames licked the painted metal, but it did not.

She turned her fingers and the knob twisted. The door popped open. She pushed it and her hands fell back to the floor. Instead of the inferno she expected to see, the hallway was clear. Her body collapsed halfway in and out of the room. The air in the hallway was clean and clear. She wiped her eyes and nose and coughed once more.

She listened for any sound, it was silent. She stood, her hand on the knob and looked back inside the room. There were no flames. There was no smoke. No wispy fireflies to guide her to clarity. No smell of smoldering oak or timber. The room was as it was when she first entered. Her lantern burned dimly, the moonlight shone through the window.

She tucked her feet back into her strappy sandals. They didn't clomp loudly because the soles were made of rubber composite. She couldn't go back in that room. Her heart began to hammer. She felt light headed. She couldn't allow herself to faint in the hallway alone, and she refused to lie on the bed.

She couldn't slow her breathing. She was in full-on panic attack mode. She didn't want to go through it by herself. She needed him–Mark was in the room next door. She didn't think he'd judge her. Her panic-stricken state wouldn't allow her to hesitate. She rushed to his door and though she intended to knock lightly, her fist pounded hard enough to wake the dead.

Chapter Nine

Ben couldn't see well in the old dusty deserted barn. He squinted and searched the shadows and corners. "Sarah!" he shouted. There was no reply. He went in further and from the corner of his eye he saw a blur of light colored clothing pass into an adjoining room. He turned and went to see what it was, "Sarah?" he called out with less confidence. This was nuts, he had just watched her come in here, he thought, why wouldn't she answer him?

He entered the next room and Sarah was at the other end, standing with her back to him. He grew frustrated with her silence and hide-and-seek games. This wasn't sexy if that's what she was going for. He walked with a fast pace until he was almost upon her. "Sarah?" he questioned, but still, she remained silent, her back still facing him, her shoulders were hunched forward. "What's wrong with you?" he asked with some irritation. He flinched when she moved.

She leaned to the right, putting all her weight on her right foot. He stopped still. Then, she leaned to the left, putting all her weight on her left foot. She shifted back to her right with a sharp motion, then sharply back to the left, right, left, right, left with strong abrupt movements. Almost unnaturally she moved in a maniacal dance.

He stared at her back and her hair as it swung and swayed back and forth, it looked longer now. Ben was getting scared. He couldn't wrap his mind around what was happening. He reached out to touch her shoulder and she spun around to face him. In terror he screamed at her twisted, contorted face. Her sunken dark eyes were black as sackcloth and the corners of her mouth were encrusted and dark veins spidered out to her cheeks. Her hair was no longer blond, but muddy black. This wasn't Sarah. She sneered at him, spread her boney fingers out and lunged at him.

Chapter Ten

Pounding on Mark's door foiled the witch's plan. Her black tendrils receded in two seconds. Like blood retreating from veins, they coiled up to the ceiling and disappeared into the hole as it shrunk back down to a tiny black dot.

Anna stood there outside Mark's door, feeling exposed to the haunts that could come at any minute. He wasn't answering her pounding. She thought, for sure, she would hear grunting and a creaking mattress coming from the room that Ben and Sarah were in, but it was actually quiet.

She balled her hand into a fist and held it two inches from Mark's door. She closed her eyes and took a deep breath. When she opened her eyes, she knocked and waited impatiently. Her stomach tightened into a frozen ball. She was just about to pound on the door when she heard his voice, "Who's there?"

She spoke through the door and called out, "It's me, Anna. Are you dressed? Can I come in?" she waited.

He quickly replied, "Yep, come on in." She soft-padded it to his bedside.

He was lying in the canopy bed, but the curtains were gone, "What's up? Are you okay?" he sounded slightly concerned.

She memorized what she saw. The image of him lying on top of the bedding, propped up with his head against the stacked pillows, in a white tee–his hoodie was on the bed next to him. His wallet and cell phone were together on the pillow next to him. It was as if she were living a fantasy romance novel and he was her lover in waiting.

Her senses returned to her, "Um, I'm too scared to stay in that room alone," she admitted robotically.

"Oh," was all he said.

"Yeah," her mind fought for a good excuse, "I think it's just too hot in there anyway. Your room is cooler than mine, more comfortable."

He sat up and scooted over on the bed and patted the comforter in invitation. Her body moved two seconds ahead of her legs in response. She hopped up on the bed, on his right. Mark picked up his wallet, cell phone and hoodie and started to get up. She blinked, "Where are you going?"

He stood and said, "Well, I was going to let you have the bed. There's a sturdy looking chair over in the corner." He took one of the pillows in his hands.

"Oh, well, you don't have to sleep in a chair. I'm sure this bed is big enough for the both of us," she offered.

Mark's stomach tightened, adrenaline shot through his chest. He was trying to be a gentleman, but she was making it very difficult. He wasn't sure she was thinking the same thing he was thinking. She sounded like she was offering something, but he didn't want to be wrong and tip the balance to something entirely misread. He squeezed the pillow and felt like he could tear it apart with all the pressure that was building in the absence of words. The air hung heavy.

She patted the mattress and he wavered. He sat back down beside her. He put the pillow against the wall and lay back to how he had been when she came in. He tried not to appear so rigid. He didn't know what to do with his hands, so he just folded them over his stomach.

"Relax," she smiled. He realized she could tell he was nervous.

He blew out a puff of air through a small smile.

"Can I ask you something?"

His eyes flashed up to her and then back to his hands he was fiddling with, "Course."

"Do you think about that conversation between us in the car?" she seemed to be holding her breath.

He nodded slightly, "Yes, I do, actually. I've been thinking about how much I enjoyed talking with you and the ride–up until the wreck anyway." and smiled.

She smiled back. He wanted things to loosen up. She bent her knee up and pulled her pant leg up to reveal three thin red lines. "Man, this really hurts." She seemed to be trying to catch his interest. She looked over at him.

She replied, "This must be from the accident or something– Or maybe I got scratched by that cat you were asking about."

"Let me look at it," he got close and wanted to get a better look but the room was dark, "Do you mind?"

She smiled and laid her leg over his lap. She was sitting on his right and it was her right leg. An image flashed through his mind of turning his body and how easily her legs would wrap around his waist. His heart pounded through him like a rock thrown into water, rippling through his chest and reverberating into his groin. He tried to focus. He turned her knee away from him so that he could inspect her cut. He pulled the lantern closer and determined in his mind that it was from no accident. There were three individual scrapes like scratches. He released her leg, but she kept it where it was.

The hole in her jeans on the front was stained with blood. It caught his eye, so he pulled her leg up to see the gash from the accident he'd seen earlier. It was red and still needed cleaning. He moved from under her leg, "Stay here, I'm gonna go check and see if I can find something to clean that wound with." He went to the adjoining bathroom. He returned with some cotton balls, rubbing alcohol, a damp rag and a box of bandages. He slipped back onto the bed and set the rag on the nightstand.

Anna placed her leg back over his lap. He pulled her knee up and it bent. He tried to wipe away the blood, but the hole wasn't big enough. He tried to use his finger wrapped in the rag, but he was unable to reach without hurting her. He sighed.

"Want me to take my jeans off?" she asked, "…So you can reach it to clean it, I mean."

He didn't know what to say, "Um, if you want to."

She stood and popped the button, unzipped and shimmied the denim down past her hips and kicked them to the foot of the bed. His eyes struggled to remain cool but her black lace, barely there, thong threatened to unravel his restraint. She seemed to be unaware of the effect she was having on him. As if being in bed, alone and only half clothed with him was no big deal. She sat back down, a black string lined her hip and attached the front to the back of her panty. Her white tank top reached just under her pierced naval.

She laid her naked leg back over him. She turned herself toward him to get more comfortable. He suddenly realized he would have to touch her and remain in control of his wandering hands. He positioned his hand to the back of her knee. She smiled at his chilled fingers. Her slender leg was soft under his touch. Her skin was darker than his, even in the low lighting. There was a faint scent of coconut that tickled his senses. He took the rag and gently wiped away the blood. She put her hand on his shoulder for balance. He put a little rubbing alcohol on a cotton ball and said, "This may hurt a little…" He blotted lightly and when she tightened her grip on his shoulder, he leaned in and blew on her knee to take the sting away.

Once the wound was clean, he un-wrapped the band aid and covered the area. "There ya go," he said. She admired his work and said, "Thank you. It feels better already. "

He asked, "What about the scratch you had on your cheek?" She turned her right cheek to the left, so he could get a better look. He examined her cheek, but it was less than an inch and as thin as a hair. He tilted her face for a better view and used a small amount of alcohol and dabbed her scratch. She was staring into his blue eyes. When she winced at the alcohol on her cheek, he leaned in and blew lightly. Then, he let go. But she didn't move away. In fact, she moved closer.

Chapter Eleven

Anna gravitated toward Mark. Like a feather, she was soft on his lips. He accepted her advance and returned in kind. With parted mouths, they lingered on each other. She reached into his hair and threaded her fingers and their kiss deepened. His soft lips were firm, they asserted their control and she moaned sweetly in response. She took his hand and placed it just above her dressed knee and he gripped gently. His hand ran up her thigh to her hip and she rewarded him with another moan of approval. She pressed into him and he leaned backward to the pillow. Her leg was still on his lap, so it didn't take much for her to be completely on top of him.

His chin tilted upwards as she kissed down his neck. Her hand glided down his shoulder and down his chest, down his abdomen to his waist. She tugged on his tee and he raised up slightly to free up the material. She ran her palm under the cotton and his skin was hot. She pulled his shirt up and he worked with her to take it off. His masculine scent and woodsy body wash filled her senses as his shirt passed by on its way to the floor.

She bent her back so that she was almost sitting up and drank in the sight of him. His cerulean eyes deepened and blinked slowly in the knowledge that she wanted him and how much he wanted her. She smiled and pulled her shirt off. He looked up at her, "I can't believe this is happening."

She smiled because she liked his humble gratitude, "Me neither. What a crazy night!"

He rolled her over onto her back and threaded his fingers to hers and kissed her deeply. An hour later, he held her close. In a tight embrace, they enjoyed the afterglow. Soon, they fell asleep in each other's arms.

Chapter Twelve

In the middle of the night, Mark lay sleeping on his back. Anna had rolled over on her side, with her back to him. The room was quiet and moonlit, peaceful. With canopy gone, the air was comfortable. Across the room the full-length mirror stood. In the reflection was the figure of a young woman, standing still, her brunette hair hung long on either side of her face.

Her eyes were dark and concentrated on the floor. She swayed slightly before she took a step forward. With one bare foot, she stepped through the glass, into the room. She was no longer a reflection but a real person. As she stood on the hardwood, she sank to the floor. On her belly, she slithered, hand over hand, until she disappeared under the bed.

The sheet grew taut as if someone was using it to pull themselves up. Mark was sound asleep. Four jagged-nailed boney fingers appeared over the side of the bed and then again with four more. Stringy hair hung long and unwashed in front of a shadowed, twisted face as her head rose above the bed.

She leaned in and hovered over Mark's body. Her head tilted to the side, curious, her face was only an inch away from his. He lay unaware and his melodic breathing was deep and restful. Her head pitched upwards slightly as she sniffed his body. Her hair fell to his face and tickled his skin.

Mark was startled from his slumber. He scratched his itchy nose and had an odd vibe. He looked around the room, but it was empty. Empty except for himself and Anna, who lay next to him. His mind drifted back to the events of earlier in the night and he wanted to hold her. He looked over at her, wanting her to be awake, yet, not wanting to wake her. She was balled up in the bed sheets, like a sexy little cocoon, all the way up over her head. She laid on her right side, facing away from him.

He decided to spoon up against her and maybe, if he rocked the bed hard enough, she would wake, and he could play innocent. He knew she would accept his advances once she was awake.

He slowly inched his way to her, carefully. He framed her body with his, her back against his front. He was in position, so he rocked the bed slightly to seem as though he were just moving around in his sleep. When she didn't stir, he rocked it a little harder. She didn't budge. He felt a little discouraged.

He leaned up and looked over her shoulder to try to see her face. The sheet was covering her too far up. She seemed so peaceful–too peaceful. He realized he didn't feel her breathing. He put his hand on her shoulder and gave her a quick shake. Her pliant body moved with his jostling but snapped right back into her original place. He grew concerned. *What if she had smothered, being wrapped so tightly?* He reached over her and pulled the sheet down but, just as he uncovered the crown of her head, he jerked his hand back. He cautiously pulled the sheet down a little further and then jumped backwards and out of the bed.

He tangled in the bedsheets and flailed his arms until he was free. He stood, his heart pounding. He stared at her limp figure still mummified and motionless. His labored breath thumped in his ears. He took a step around the foot of the bed and her body jolted and then came back into her silence. He could see her though she was swaddled. He reluctantly took another step and she suddenly rolled off the side of the bed and disappeared from his sight.

Mark stumbled backwards and regained his balance. 'Where did she go?' he asked himself. 'Where was Anna?' That certainly wasn't her. When he had pulled the sheet down, he saw black hair and Anna's hair wasn't that dark.

He backed up for fear the thing would be under the bed. He tried to stretch up onto the balls of his feet to get a look on the other side of the bed, but he was too far away. He grabbed his boxers and tee and got dressed and slipped on his jeans, hoodie and shoes. He knelt to see under the bed when he heard the floor creak. He got back to his feet and began to back up until he was pressed firmly to the door.

The floor creaked again, and he couldn't take his eyes off the bed. He fully anticipated her to crawl out from her hiding. He imagined her creeping along the floorboards, hand over hand, maniacally. But instead he saw motion at the corner of his eye and quickly sought what he saw.

There, in the full-length mirror, stood a narrow figure, clothed in a long white nightgown, long black hair covered her face as she slouched. His eyes were frozen on her as he reached down for the door knob. When he couldn't find it easily, he reached with both hands. She took a step from the mirror into the room and he ripped at the door knob and ran out into the hallway.

He opened the door to the whispering room and looked inside, no Ben and no Sarah. He slammed the door and asked, "Where IS everyone?! What's going on?!"

He went to the room with the cats and, when he didn't see Anna, he ran down the corridor and down the stairs. He searched the dark rooms for a familiar face. He rounded the corner and skidded to a stop. At the end of the hall stood a man he didn't know. He was standing, facing the open basement doorway. And, he was holding Anna's unconscious body. Mark held one hand out in plea, but the man took one step and the darkness enveloped them.

Mark ran to the basement door and strained to see into the inky blackness. He couldn't hear the man's footsteps either. He still had the matches in his pocket, so he turned and saw a lantern on a decorating table. He grabbed it and lit it and stepped down–down into the inky-black basement.

~*~

Chapter Thirteen

Mark reached the bottom of the stairs. It was black as night and the glow from his lantern was as weak as a birthday candle in a sunless cavern. Shadows seemed to take life, luminous and threatening. He held the lantern out in front of him and moved it in a half circle, illuminating a little at a time as he walked. He wished he had a weapon. He felt vulnerable and unarmed. He kept his head on a swivel. He wanted to call out for her, but he didn't want to call attention to himself–even though he lit himself up. He maneuvered around the stacks of boxes and old stored furniture.

He heard nothing of the man, nor of Anna–not even a creak or whimper. He rounded a dividing wall and bumped into another tall mirror. He jumped and let out a breath of relief. He turned and saw her, just an arm. It was hanging limp over the side of a gurney style table. His heart skipped a beat, and, in its absence, the pounding echoed in his ears.

He stared at her pale limb as it hung motionless. He swiped the room with his eyes, fearing it was a trap. He didn't care though, he had to help her. He swiftly crept up to her arm. Looking behind him and all around, he touched her hand. It was ice cold and a little stiff. His heart pounded in his chest. He ran his fingers down to her wrist and felt for a pulse, there was none. The pounding deafened him, and his stomach turned.

She couldn't be…dead. Yet, she showed no signs of life.

He began to breathe heavy. He had to take her body from this place. He set the lantern down by her shoulder. His heart began to ache. He couldn't protect her. Just a short time ago they were wrapped in each other, moving against each other and her warm body was on fire for him– pressed into him, rubbing and riding him in rhythmic response. Now her rigid frame would never again be warm.

He leaned his ear down to her chest and strained in desperate hope for one faint heartbeat but heard only silent report. She was really gone. He struggled to get his mind around this but to no avail. Pain filled him, loss and sorrow all at once. He wanted to gather her in his arms and hold her, regardless of the fact that she was dead. He got closer to her and scooped her up with the idea that he would carry her out. He couldn't leave her here. As he pulled her up, he saw her face. Then he let her drop and jolted backwards into a stack of books sitting dusty on a vanity.

Her face was frozen in fear, twisted, with her mouth gaping and the corners of her mouth were stretched and torn. Blood was crusted on her chin. It was gruesome, but it wasn't Anna. It was Sarah! He fought for his balance and grabbed for the lantern. He held it out in front of him and lit Sarah's contorted expression. Confusion clouded his vision and fled just as rapidly. He didn't understand why Sarah was down here and why she was dead. Also, he couldn't understand how or why she made the face she did. What had she seen that scared her so?

But mostly, he realized that if this was Sarah's body, where was Anna? If that man had brought Sarah down here and she was dead, it was only a matter of time before the same thing happened to Anna. He raised the lantern and examined the room. His newfound courage blinded him to fear. There was still hope. He frantically searched. At the back wall of the room was a weathered wooden door with white chipped paint. He tried the knob and it opened. He pushed the door and it swung easily all the way and bumped into the cement wall. He was prepared to charge in through the doorway. The room was small and, in the light of the lantern, stood the farmer, only three feet in front of him, facing him, holding Anna's slender comatose form in his arms.

Mark was startled and yelped at the sudden sight of them so close to him. He twisted his body away as if he had been physically shoved, then straightened and faced the farmer when he realized he wasn't going to attack. He stared at the large, plaid clad burly ghost of a man. His shoulders were hunched, and his haunted face was locked onto Anna's unconscious countenance. He held her like she was his; as if his grief was unknown to anyone else.

Mark was afraid to move, afraid to disrupt the situation, afraid it would turn ugly. But he couldn't let him hurt her. When he had thought she was dead, it was almost too much for him to bear. Now that there was still time to save her, he wouldn't let him have her.

"Hey," Mark finally mustered, "please…give her to me."

The farmer didn't react. Mark swallowed hard and reasserted, "Please, whoever you are, hand her to me." The farmer stood, swaying slightly for long moments as Mark sought for the right words. Then the farmer spoke, "My child, forgive me." His eyes were two black pools, deep and pained. They cried black tears down his cheeks. Mark tried to think of what to say but the farmer re-pitched his plea. "My sweet little girl, I didn't mean to…" his voice trailed off. Mark watched as the tormented spirit confessed his sins to Anna's limp body.

The farmer fought with his grief, "I didn't want to kill you, my little girl. You were just…bad." Then, he lowered her to her concrete floor and, with one hand, he held her shoulders up. In his other hand he held a large knife. He raised the blade high. Mark's wide eyes and pounding heart threw his adrenaline into overdrive. He rushed for the farmer. Just as the blade came down, Mark's shoulder blocked and rammed into the burly man. The farmer vanished. The only thing left of him was his blade that was stuck in Mark's bicep.

Mark grabbed the handle, pulled it out and threw it across the room in anger at how much it hurt. He picked Anna up and leaned his head down to her chest, still beating. She was alive. He carried her upstairs and laid her on a couch. He ripped a long piece of material from the bottom of his t-shirt and tied it around his wound. He brushed her cheek with his hand and she flinched. Her eyes squinted open and she looked at him, confusion on her face.

Mark smiled, "You're okay?"

She let her eyes drift around the dark room. "Where am I?" she asked.

"We are on the first floor, in the living room." he explained.

That didn't clarify anything for her, he realized "What are we doing down here? Weren't we upstairs in bed? How did we get down here?" She rambled off questions faster than Mark could answer. He tried anyway, "We were in bed, but something is going on in this house. This place is haunted."

"I know. I had some things happen to me too," she admitted.

"You have had something happen, what?" he asked.

"Earlier, when you got stuck in the floor, I was locked in the room Ben and Sarah are sleeping in. The door wasn't locked but it wouldn't open. There was whispering and these old dolls and that mirror in our room, I thought I saw a man standing there." She rambled on and her fear was heavy in her voice.

"It's okay," he comforted her. "I saw cats under the bed when I was stuck in the floor. I heard them and when I put my hand in the hole in the floor, I felt them against my hand. Their eyes kept multiplying. It wasn't possible."

She sat up and looked around the room. "So, let's get out of here. I don't care about the car. Let's just get Ben and Sarah and start running."

He resituated the makeshift bandage on his arm and said, "Listen, don't get upset," he cautioned, "I can't find Ben, he wasn't in the room. But I did find Sarah."

"Well, did she know where Ben was?" she asked.

"No, um, she was dead."

"Dead?!" she exclaimed.

"Shh, yes, she was dead, in the basement. And when I found you, you were unconscious in the arms of a man. Er,…the ghost of a man."

"What man?!" she questioned.

"I don't know but I think he killed his daughter here. I think he thought you were his daughter. He was going to stab you. When I shoved into him, he just…disappeared."

"What? Stab me? Are you serious?" she hugged herself.

"Yes, he had a knife. But he wound up stabbing me instead." He indicated to his seeping arm.

She shot up to the edge of the couch and pulled his arm closer to inspect it. "Oh my gosh, are you okay?"

He nodded, "I'll be okay. It doesn't hurt as much as I thought it would, actually."

She replied, "We must get you looked at."

"Well, we need that jack and tire iron, so we can drive to where I can get it looked at. I don't think I can walk for too long," he said.

She stood and offered, "Do you want to lie down?"

"No," he shook his head, "but we need to think where to find what we need. Maybe we should try the barn?"

"I guess, sure. I'll follow you."

~*~

They left through the front door and walked around the side of the towering home. It was a dark night, and they kept their eyes ahead of them. Anna took his hand. She wanted to make sure they stuck together this time. It wasn't too hard to find the barn even through the tall corn.

They reached the barn door and Mark pulled it open with some effort since his arm was injured. It was still bleeding. He went in first. It wasn't anything spectacular, nothing too out of the ordinary. With the strange goings-on in the house, she half expected a barrage of spinning specters, glowing ghosts and orbiting orbs square dancing to the ceiling. But all was quiet.

They searched for anything automotive at all. They walked the length and back before crossing into the next room. It was full length, just as the side they had just covered. There were no horses either. As they entered the doorway, Mark was jerked up off his feet, hovered for a second, and then flew backwards, landing on his back in the hay. Anna turned to see him land just before the door slammed in front of her, parting them once again.

Anna heard a woman's laughter and she turned in all directions for its origin. She pulled on the door, but it remained firm. She felt a fingernail scratch on her bare arm and she swirled around but there was nothing there. She felt another scratch on her cheek and covered her face. She sought the room frantically for someone to fight. Then another thin burning line formed on her forearm, spilling her crimson blood.

"What do you want?!" she shouted.

Nothing was the reply.

"What do you want from me?!"

From behind her, she heard, "To die!"

Anna swirled around and saw the twisted face branding a twisted sneer and holding a pitchfork pointed right at Anna's stomach. The ghost spirit-charged toward her and Anna grabbed both hands around the talons. They rushed backwards until they ran out of room. Anna's back hit the wall and she pushed the fork to the side far enough that the fork speared the wall, only grazing her.

The maniacal girl smiled and held one boney finger up. She pivoted it side-to-side in a no-no-no gesture. Anna side-stepped past her, keeping herself facing the girl. She wouldn't turn her back to the creature. She wasn't watching where she was going and tripped over something. She fell over what felt like a bag of sand. She quickly tried to get back to her feet when she realized it was no bag of sand.

Her hands balanced on the shoulder of what remained of Ben. His cold, stiff body lay rigid on his side, in fetal position. His face was frozen in fear, locked in a stretched-out scream. His mouth and jaw were so wide that they must have been unhinged. Anna jumped back and shuffled backwards. The demon girl seemed to enjoy her response and cocked her head sideways like a dog does. She stared down at her ensnared prey. But Anna had other plans, she gathered her senses, jumped to her feet and ran back toward the door.

The ghastly girl gave chase, wailing all the way to the door, but Anna came to a halt, turned and faced her nemesis and she stopped. Anna stood bravely, unwavering. The girl lifted her lips and bared her teeth. Anna narrowed her eyes and her nose twitched at the rotten smell that was enveloping her.

"Your daddy won't be happy if you keep hurting people," Anna tried.

The girl's lips slowly sealed back over her gritty teeth.

"Your daddy will have to discipline you again if you keep this up."

The girl flinched.

"I know, he told me so when I saw him in the basement," Anna lied.

The girl bent her neck and brought her ear down to her shoulder, in a childlike manner.

It was working! "He's getting rather angry because he likes me. You don't want to hurt me and make him mad, do you?" The girl's eyes shifted back and forth as if trying to think of a way to escape punishment.

"So, I'm just going to open this door and leave, and you won't be in trouble," she turned to the door but kept her eyes on the spirit. She pushed the door and it opened. Mark backed up and, with one hand over his wound, he held the other out for Anna.

Anna walked through the doorway, took Mark's hand and they both walked calmly toward the barn's exit like they were walking away from a rabid Pit Bull, trying not to show fear. Mark saw the dark, angry girl and was confused about what had just happened and why they were being allowed to leave.

When the girl saw Mark, she grew hungry. Men were her weakness and she wanted to play with him. They heard a loud shriek behind them and saw her running after them with her hands out in front of her. They bolted. As they ran out the front door, the girl's nails swiped Mark's back, but they were free.

Chapter Fourteen

They kept running, hand in hand. Through the corn they stayed straight. Mark caught a glimpse of a small building and he turned their direction. They slowed down in front of a small shed. Anna bent over, her hands on her hips, and tried to catch her breath. Mark peered into one of the barred windows of the shed to see what it held. He walked around to the door and jiggled the handle, locked. He went around to the other side and looked in the window that was also strangely barred.

There, against the wall, laid a small jack. On the wall, hanging from a nail, among other tools, was a tire iron. He found a large rock in the dirt and threw it at the window. Anna jumped. The glass broke, and he carefully removed the hanging jagged pieces. He pushed against the bars, but they were fixed, they weren't going anywhere.

"We have to get in this shed!" Mark declared.

Anna stood straight and went to the window. She stood on her tip-toes to see inside. She saw the jack and tire iron and agreed, "Definitely." She looked at the handle. Yes, it was locked but something familiar was stuck in the keyhole. She pried it out with her fingernail.

"What is it?" Mark asked.

"It's a bent bottle cap," she identified.

"Okay, so why was it stuck in the keyhole?" he wondered.

He rested his back on the door, suddenly feeling a little weak and tired.

"I don't know but I have seen this before… in the house. I couldn't sleep so I went through the dresser. There was a drawer with a bunch of keys in it. One of them had a bottle cap bent around it…" she trailed off.

"Really?" Mark queried. He shut his eyes for a moment and he felt dizzy. He let his back slip down the door and his butt landed on the ground. Anna looked down at him, "Are you okay?"

Mark squinted up at her, "I've been better," he said weakly.

She knelt in front of him, "Okay, this is what's gonna happen: I know where the key is to this door. We need it and you are too weak to go. I'm going back to the farmhouse and I'm gonna get the key and I will be right back."

He wanted to tell her no and that he would go instead, or at least go with her. But he was lightheaded, and the starry night was swirling above him. "Listen, please be careful. Just run in quick and run back out. Got it?" he asserted himself. She agreed. She stood so that she could see the farmhouse. She fell back to her knees and kissed his lips. Then she was running through the corn alone.

Chapter Fifteen

Anna tried to be quiet as she opened the front door. She left it open and crept up the stairs. As she made her way to the room with the hole in the floor, she felt hopeful that all would remain uneventful. She was glad the lanterns were all still lit. She slowly opened the bedroom door and quickly crossed the room. She wasted no time as she sifted through the drawer until she found the key with the bottle cap bent around it. She stuffed it in her pocket and turned to leave.

She stuck her head out into the hallway and it was empty. She let out a sign of relief and stepped out into the open. She crept a few steps when she heard a male voice. He whimpered a grieving groan. It was getting louder. He was coming up the stairs. She panicked and pushed through the closest door to her and it was the one on her right.

She cringed when she realized she was back in the whispering room. All three dolls were still perched politely on the dresser. But, the room was alive–bright points of light shot across the room. Orbs bounced around like fireflies. It was like a 3D planetarium from another plane. She marveled at the ceiling.

The whispering was like a soundtrack, loud, but still too many voices to differentiate one from another. She watched in awe as the orbs flew up to her, zipped back and forth, and shot away into the corners. One circled her head. She kept her eye on it like Godzilla watched the tiny helicopter as it flew around her. One danced in front of her face and landed on her shoulder.

She heard its tiny voice as it sang to her, "The mirror…you can get outside through the mirror…they use it to come and go." It flittered away but returned to her other shoulder. It hovered close to her ear and sang once again, "Use the mirror…but be quick. Just walk through it, don't look back…hurry, he's coming!"

She felt her breath flee from her as fear took its place. The little orb had warned her that he was coming. She twisted around to the knob and it opened this time. She cracked it slightly and peeked out. She saw the farmer at the top of the stairway. He wasn't moving. She needed to get to the room across the hall. She contemplated making a break for it, but she wasn't sure she trusted the little firelight.

She waited and watched him. He began to move. The dancing light flickered across his face. Anna covered her mouth to keep from screaming–he had no eyes! His sockets were empty and black streaks stained his cheeks as though his grief permanently disfigured his face. He stepped toward her even though he hadn't seen her. She felt her heart pound. He took another step but then turned into the bathroom.

She seized the opportunity and did a soft, quick paced run across the hardwood to the door. She closed it behind her and let out another sigh of relief. She saw the mirror to her left. She started toward it when she stopped and went to the bedside table. She took the alcohol, cotton and bandages Mark had used on her gash and stuffed it all in her jeans wherever it would fit. On the floor lay her white slouch-sweater. She grabbed it and pulled it over her head. Then she picked up the flickering lantern and went to the mirror. She stood in front of it, afraid of what she would see reflected in it.

To her relief, it was just her. She frowned. She was a mess, she realized. As she stood there, she thought about Mark. She wasn't sure how the mirror worked or if it even was what the orb had said. She reached out and knocked on the image of herself. She felt silly, "I'm going crazy. People don't walk through mirrors and talk to fireflies."

Maybe it was a trap. But she was worried about Mark. She thought of how weak he looked when she left him by the shed. She just wanted to get back to him as soon as possible. The mirror shimmied. Her reflection quivered like a cup of water in a dinosaur movie. The colors of her image changed from grey and white into shades of green and black. As the quaking vision simmered and fell still, her image no longer remained.

Instead, she was standing in front of a framed view of tall corn stalks, dirt floor, starry skyscape, the small shed and...Mark. She couldn't believe what she was seeing. Behind her she heard the door creaking open. The farmer was coming!

Her eyes scanned the mirror for a way to make it work. As the door slowly opened behind her, one tiny pin of light flew in fast. It spun in front of her and said, "Just go through it! Go! Go now!" It practically shouted at her. She listened and stepped into it. Her mind spiraled and everything encircled her in a blur, like a real-life jigsaw, she became part of the spinning mass. She felt like she was floating in a sea of nothingness. Falling yet going nowhere.

She was being pulled from within, broken down and reassembled. She thought, *this must be what it's like getting beamed down in a sci-fi movie. Shuffled like a deck of cards.*

Then, it stopped. She was standing alone in the middle of sweet-scented corn and clean earthy soil. She looked around and located the towering farmhouse–it was far from her now. The mirror was gone. She pointed herself on the right path and ran for the shed.

Chapter Sixteen

Mark was drifting in and out; his heavy lids were no match for gravity tonight. Loss of blood didn't help. He was only worried about her though. She had been gone too long. He heard footsteps and his head fell in their direction. She emerged from the shadows and he sighed. She was okay, and it wasn't the creepy farmer or his daughter. She dropped in front of him and took his face in her hands, "Hey, you okay?" She forced him to look into her eyes.

"I'm still here, babe," he half-smiled, reassuringly. She smirked and emptied her pockets. She un-wrapped his stab wound and clenched her teeth sympathetically. She hissed as she drew in her breath.

"That doesn't sound good," he said without the strength for humor.

She used the alcohol to clean the blood around the puncture and used the clean cotton and bandages to cover it and tossed his torn t-shirt. She pulled out the cap-covered key and unlocked the shed. Mark sat up, so she could get in. She unhooked the tire iron and grabbed the jack and returned to him.

"Okay, this is it. We have what we need. You have to help me, I can't carry you," she said.

Mark nodded and gathered his strength. He stood shakily, and she got under his good arm. She handed him the tire iron and he bent his fingers around it as it hung at his side.

She strung her arm through the jack and used her hands to hold his arm around her. He balanced on her but didn't put all his weight on her.

They managed to clear the corn and the earth turned to gravel beneath their feet. As they passed the familiar tree stump, he imagined the snaggley cat jumping up to scare him as it did before, but it did not. They crossed the old country road, but the car was at least half a mile up the road. They took it easy but hurried as Mark was still losing blood. They found the car. Mark helped her get the car up on the jack and, eventually, they got the tire changed. She looked at Mark with nervous eyes, "Mark, tell me you have the keys."

Mark slouched on a rock as he said, "This is Ben's car. He has the keys." A look of defeat filled her eyes and she slammed her fist against the top of the car.

"That's it! I'm friggin' done! C'mon!" she yelled.

She kicked the spare tire, "Even if I break the window and get in, I can't start it!"

They stumbled to the side of the asphalt and she helped him sit. A car was coming up the road, so she stood in the middle and when a pristine 1974 Eldorado Cadillac convertible came close, she waved her arms. The car crept to a standstill. Mark watched as she went to the driver and pleaded with the old man for help. He was at least in his eighties and white haired. Mark saw him nod and she came back and helped him up. They hobbled to the Cadillac and she opened the backseat door. She helped him in and slipped in beside him.

The old, metal beast began to roll and the self-proclaimed great, great grandfather of four seemed to enjoy the company. "So, what are you two young-ins doing out so early in the morning?"

He was just happy to be mobile. "Our car wrecked, and we can't get it started," he summed it up. He glanced at her in the rearview mirror. He was aware of how rough they both looked but he figured the car wreck excuse would be plausible.

"We could really use a hospital, sir, is it far?" she asked.

"Oh, it's not too far, only 'bout ten minutes from here."

She pulled Mark's weary head against her shoulder and he rested his eyes. "Thank you so much," she sounded sincere. The old man smiled, "Don't worry about it, sweetheart. You're just lucky you flagged me down. I don't usually drive this way. I reckon it's been years since I've come this way."

Mark asked faintly, "You're not from around here?"

The old driver adjusted the rearview mirror to see Mark, "Yes, I live nearby, but..." he paused, "I don't drive by the Jensen's farmhouse property anymore."

He stiffened, "What do you mean?" he asked.

The old man tipped his head but kept his eyes on the road. "There was a farmer that lived there with his daughter. She was a bit...friendly, you might say. Gentlemen callers would come and go at all times of the night when her father was out of town. Some would come but never go. Men passing through, hitchhikers and wanderers who fell for her temptation would disappear without a trace, or maybe they just got what they wanted and stayed their path. Rumors circulated about her. We should have listened–Robbie and I. Robbie was my best friend and she took him from all of us." He looked up in the mirror at them and shifted his hat, "It was his birthday. I haven't talked about him in almost sixty years." He was visibly shaken.

Anna put a hand on his boney shoulder, "I'm so sorry for your loss. What happened to him?"

The old man smiled sympathetically at her reflection behind him, "They never found him. And it wasn't long after that the house burned down to the ground. The barn was still there last I saw twenty years ago, but the house is gone."

At that moment, they rode past the old farmhouse. Just as the old timer had said, the farmhouse they had just survived, and lost two friends, was not there. It wasn't standing tall, ominous and haunting. It was an overgrown field, a dilapidated barn, a collapsed shed and broken pieces of wood sticking up through tall grass. The path leading up to the house was hidden.

Anna shivered against Mark as his skin turned to gooseflesh. She squeezed Mark tighter and the two could only hug each other tightly and stare out the window as they coasted past.

Anna blew out a sign of relief as a road sign with the large letter 'H' came into view indicating the hospital wasn't far. They turned into the emergency lane. The old man had said they were lucky. 'Lucky', Mark thought to herself, they'd had no idea how lucky they were.

Coming soon:

Shadow Princes Series

Shadow Princes: The Silver Papyrus

Prince D'arian is tired of losing to the powerful, exotic Shadow Princes. In his attempt to harness their power for himself he accidentally pulls unsuspecting beauty, Rayne Thomas, into his dimension. Can she avoid the handsome yet dangerous Shadow Prince, Nick? Or will she find that the bad guy isn't so bad after all? Rayne must keep from becoming a prisoner in a foreign land, defend her realm from those that seek to invade it and protect her unguarded heart. Can she ever go back home? Will she even want to? Coming soon in print and eBook!